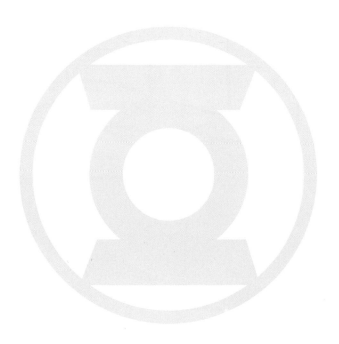

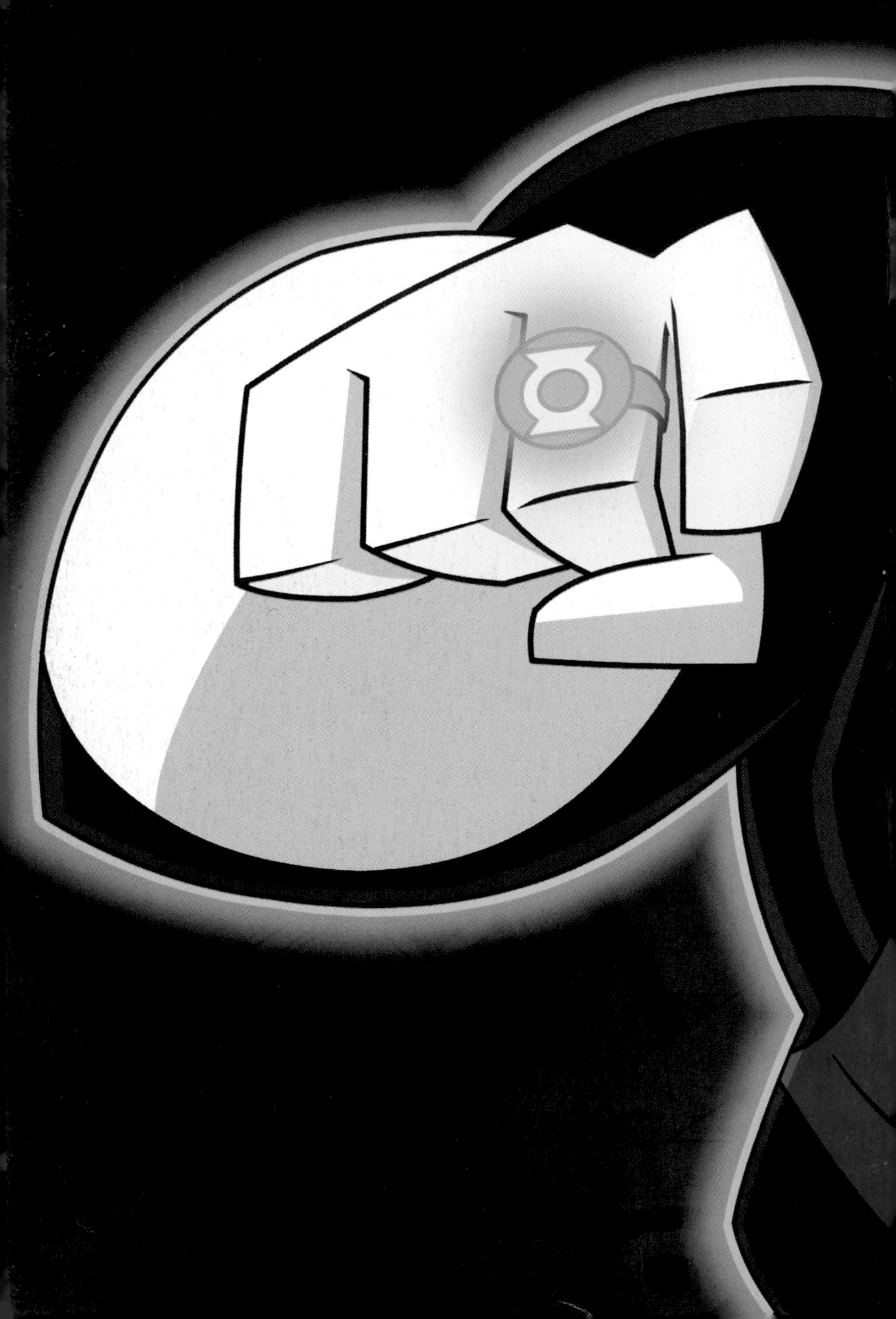

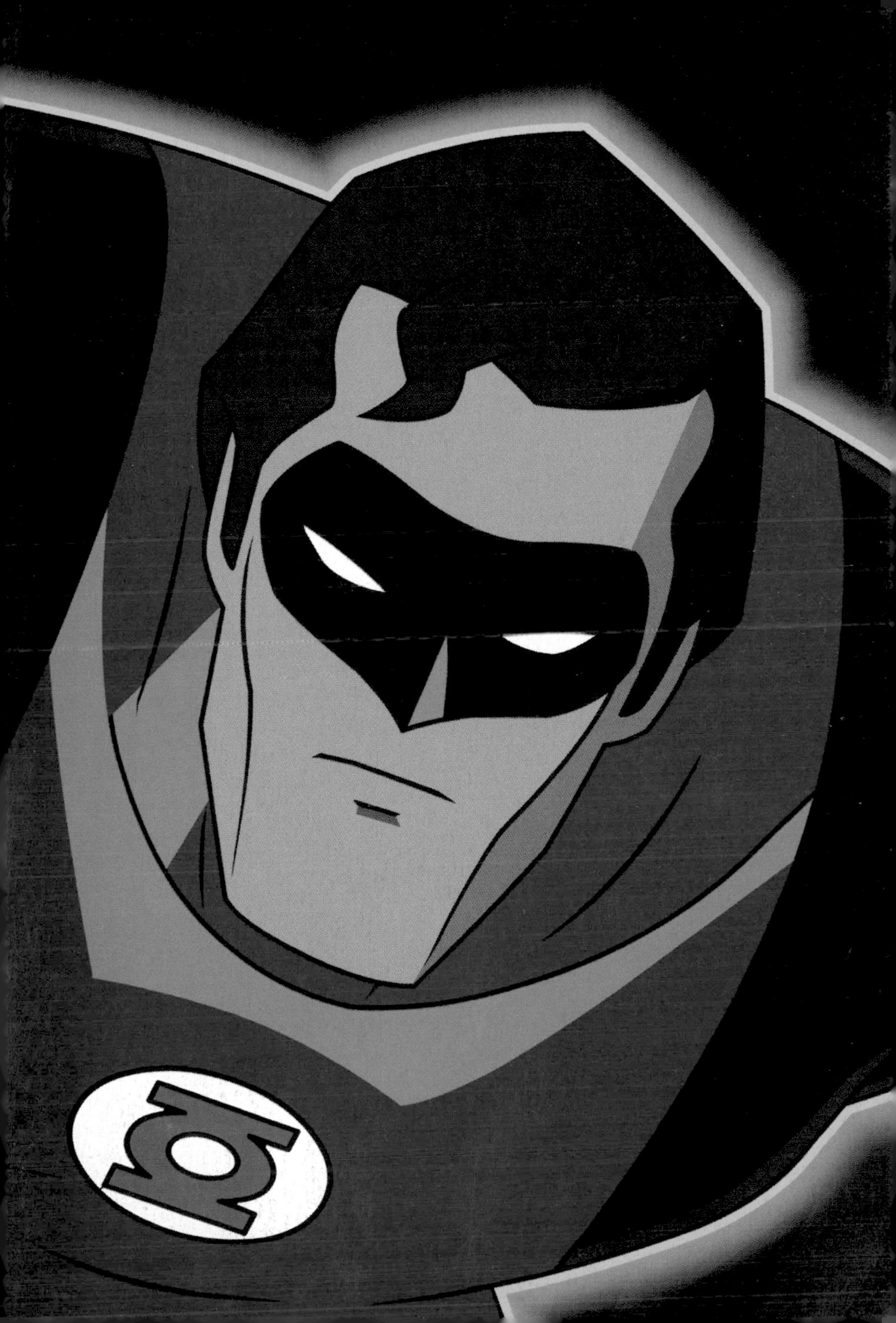

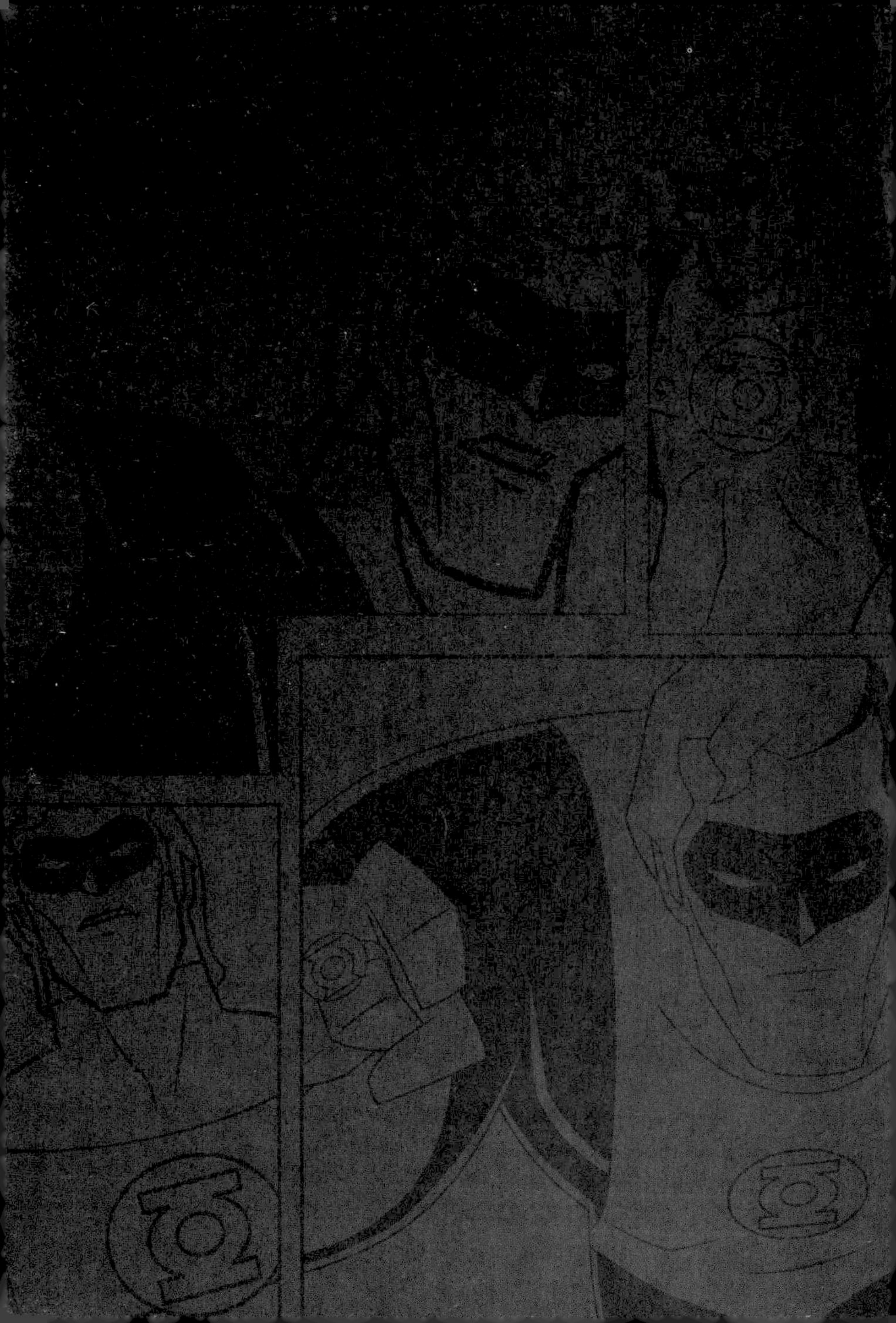

AS THE NEWEST MEMBER OF AN INTERGALACTIC PEACEKEEPING
FORCE KNOWN AS THE GREEN LANTERN CORPS, HAL JORDAN
FIGHTS EVIL AND PROUDLY WEARS THE UNIFORM AND RING OF . . .

SUPER DC HEROES

GREEN LANTERN

THE LIGHT KING STRIKES!

WRITTEN BY
LAURIE S. SUTTON

ILLUSTRATED BY
DAN SCHOENING

STONE ARCH BOOKS
a capstone imprint

Published by Stone Arch Books in 2011
A Capstone Imprint
151 Good Counsel Drive, P.O. Box 669
Mankato, Minnesota 56002
www.capstonepub.com

Library of Congress Cataloging-in-Publication Data

Sutton, Laurie.
  The Light King strikes! / written by Laurie Sutton ; illustrated by Dan
Schoening.
     p. cm. -- (DC super heroes. Green Lantern)
  ISBN 978-1-4342-2610-5 (library binding) -- ISBN 978-1-4342-3083-6 (pbk.)
  1. Graphic novels. [1. Graphic novels. 2. Superheroes--Fiction.] I. Schoening,
Dan, ill. II. Title.
  PZ7.7.S87Lig 2011
  741.5'973--dc22   2010025599

Summary: After patrolling the galaxy, Hal Jordan, a member of the Green
Lantern Corps, streaks toward Earth and the neon lights of Las Vegas.
Suddenly, the brightest city on the planet goes dark! Touching down, Hal
spots the source of the blackout . . . the evil Dr. Light! He'll stop at nothing to
absorb all the light in the universe and become the most powerful villain ever.
Hal must put an end to this light king's reign, or it'll be lights out for him as
well.

Art Director: Bob Lentz
Designer: Hilary Wacholz
Production Specialist: Michelle Biedscheid

Printed in the United States of America in Stevens Point, Wisconsin.
082011
006341R

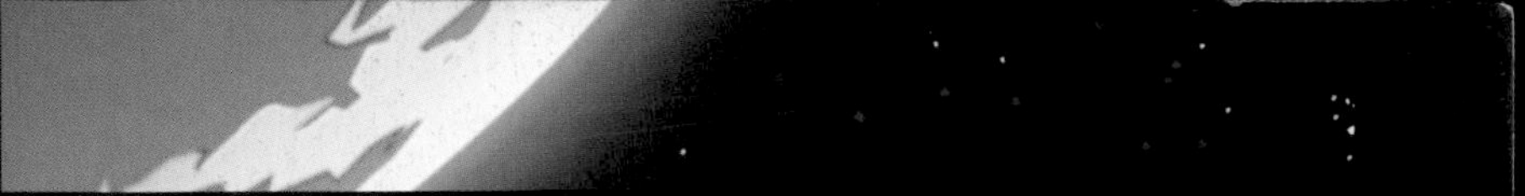

TABLE OF CONTENTS

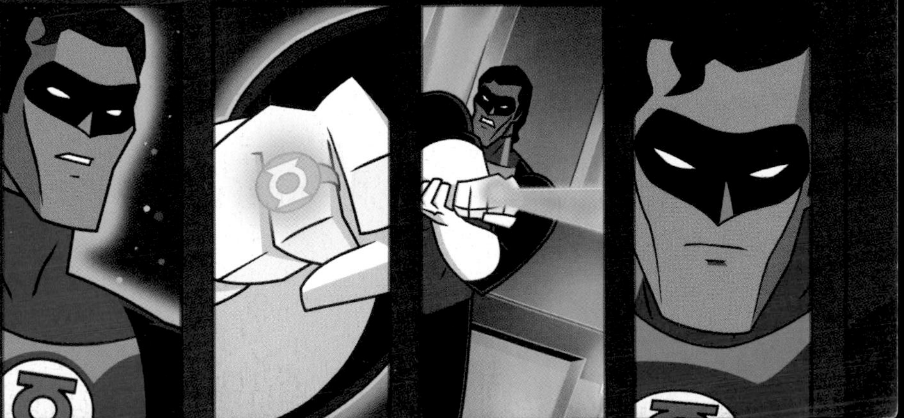

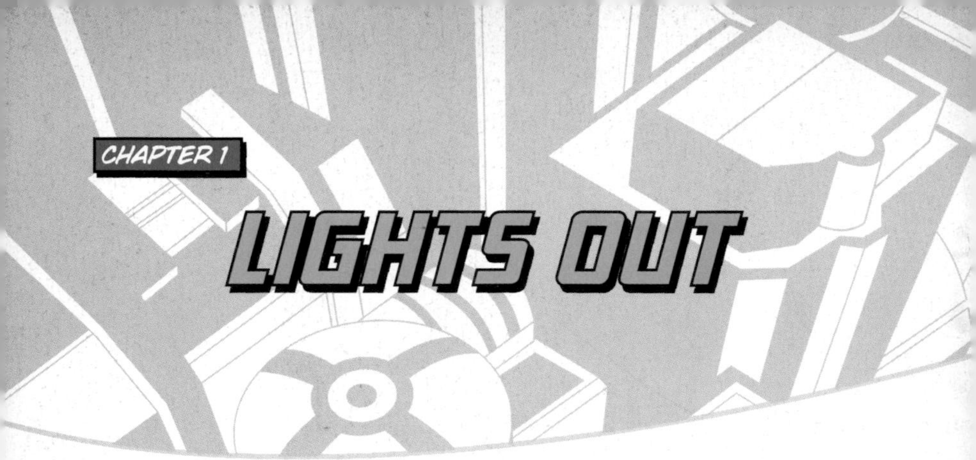

CHAPTER 1

LIGHTS OUT

Hal Jordan flew past the moon on his way home to Earth. He was finished with his patrol of Space Sector 2814 at last. It was his job to monitor the planets in this section of space. The Guardians of the Universe had given him this duty when he first became a member of the Green Lantern Corps.

He was close now. With the night side of the blue planet facing him, Hal could see the lights of many cities across the United States. One glowed brighter than them all.

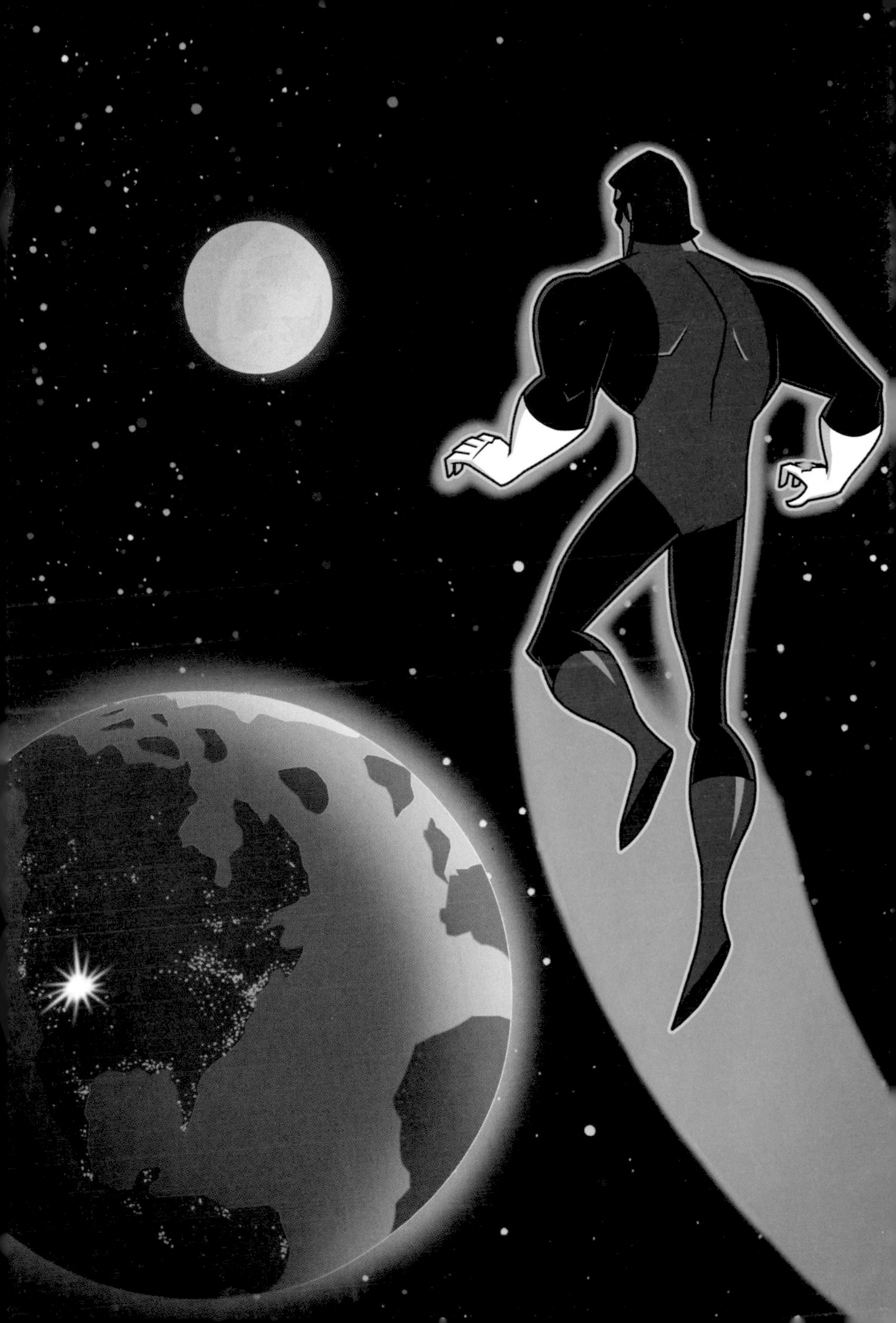

"Las Vegas," Hal said to himself, recognizing the brightest city on Earth.

Then suddenly, the lights of Las Vegas began to disappear. Green Lantern watched them dim and go out.

"A blackout!" the super hero shouted. Hal knew thousands and thousands of people were in that city. He knew they must be in danger.

His special power ring did whatever Green Lantern's willpower commanded it to do. Right now, Hal willed it to get him to Las Vegas — and fast. ZWWWOOOOMMMM!

The Apollo astronauts took three days to travel from the moon to Earth. Green Lantern did it in one minute.

On the ground, the city was so dark that Hal could not see very far.

All the lights on all the buildings were out. The streetlights were out. Even the headlights on the cars were out. The super hero heard people calling for help, but he couldn't see them.

"I need to shed a little light on this problem," said the super hero.

Hal formed a picture in his mind, and instantly the power ring made it real. The super hero created four giant light bulbs out of the ring's green energy. They floated in the sky above the city and lit it up. Everything looked green, but now Green Lantern could see where he was needed.

High atop one of the tallest buildings, Hal spotted a roller coaster. It had been built twenty stories above the ground. When the power went out, the ride came to a halt, trapping passengers onboard.

Green Lantern willed his ring to form a giant basket. **WHOOOOSH!**

"Hop in, folks!" he told the frightened riders. "I'll lower you to safety!"

As soon as Hal placed them gently on the ground, he was off to another emergency. Another ride had gone haywire. This time, a huge Ferris wheel had stopped spinning. Fearful passengers were stuck high in the air.

Green Lantern quickly formed two giant robotic hands. Then he used the mechanical limbs to pick the passengers from their seats, on by one, and set them down on the ground.

"Thank you, Green Lantern," said a man, nearly crying with fear. "I was getting dizzy on that thing!"

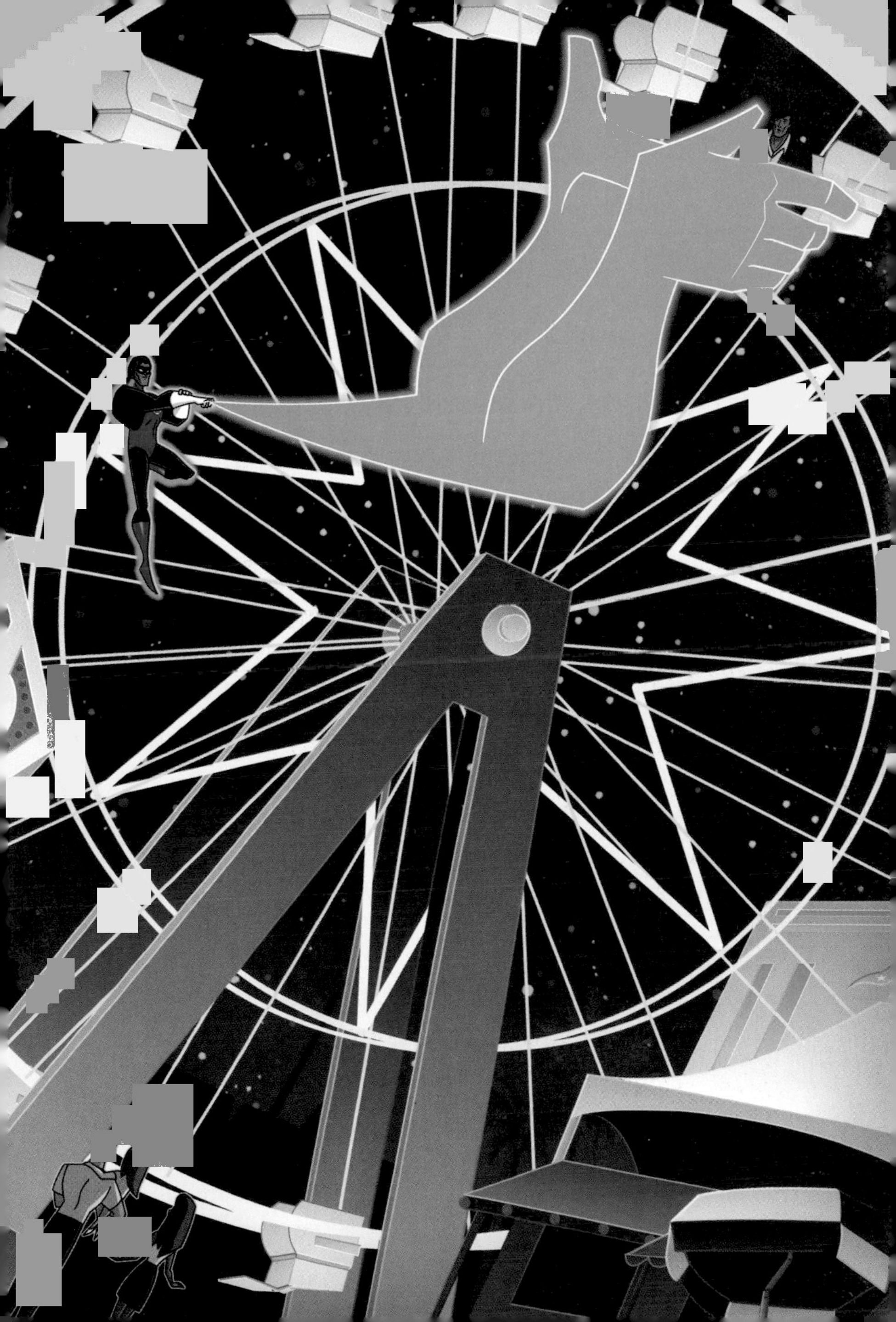

"Hey, dad, you look green," said his son. "Are you going to be sick?"

Green Lantern pointed up at the emerald-colored light bulbs in the sky.

"Everyone is going to be a little green until I can find out what's causing the blackout —" the super hero explained.

Suddenly, Green Lantern heard crashes in the distance.

"Uh-oh," he said. "Sounds like trouble."

A few seconds later, Green Lantern located the source of the disturbance. Robbers were trying to escape with cash and poker chips from one of the hotel casinos. Their getaway car was driving down the wrong side of the main street.

All the traffic lights were out. No one knew when to stop or go. Before a horrible car accident could occur, Hal had to stop the robbers from getting away.

"If those thieves want money," said the super hero, "I'll give them a ton of it!"

The power ring turned Green Lantern's imagination into reality. A gigantic stack of glowing green cash dropped on top of the getaway car. The weight stopped the car in its tracks.

CRUNCH! The roof pressed in on the robbers so they couldn't get out.

"That will hold them until the police arrive," Green Lantern said.

Although he had stopped the thieves, Hal still didn't have an explanation for why the lights went out in Las Vegas.

Green Lantern knew if he found the answer to that question, he would be able to restore the power.

"Locate the source of the power failure in this city," he told the power ring.

The rings worn by the Green Lantern Corps were known to be the most powerful weapons in the universe. They were also very powerful computers.

"Negative," the ring quickly responded. "There is no power failure."

"But all the lights are out!" Green Lantern exclaimed. "What else could cause the blackout?"

"I'm detecting an unusual energy signature," the ring answered. "Calculating location . . ."

Moments later, a green map of downtown Las Vegas appeared in front of Green Lantern. A glowing X flashed in the middle of the map.

"Ring, identify this energy signature," Green Lantern commanded.

"It is human in origin," the ring said. "This human goes by the name of . . . Dr. Light."

CHAPTER 2

DUEL IN THE DARK

"Dr. Light!" Green Lantern shouted with anger. "Of course! I've battled that small-time crook before. He must have control of the city's light spectrum."

Green Lantern followed the map to a large hotel shaped like a pyramid. A brilliant beam of light shot up from the top of the building. A person stood in the middle of the beam. Green Lantern could not see who it was because of the glare, but he knew it had to be Dr. Light.

The beam faded to black. Dr. Light had soaked up the energy like a sponge.

"So you're the cause of this blackout," Hal shouted toward the villain. "You absorbed all the light in the city."

"I plan to do more than that," Dr. Light replied, flying quickly away. "And you will never stop me!"

"We'll see about that," said Hal.

A ribbon of green energy flowed out of the super hero's power ring and then multiplied into a dozen steel strands. The strands formed cage bars around Dr. Light.

"Ha! Is that all you've got?" Dr. Light asked with a laugh. "I've already absorbed the light power of the brightest city on Earth, and I know how to use it!"

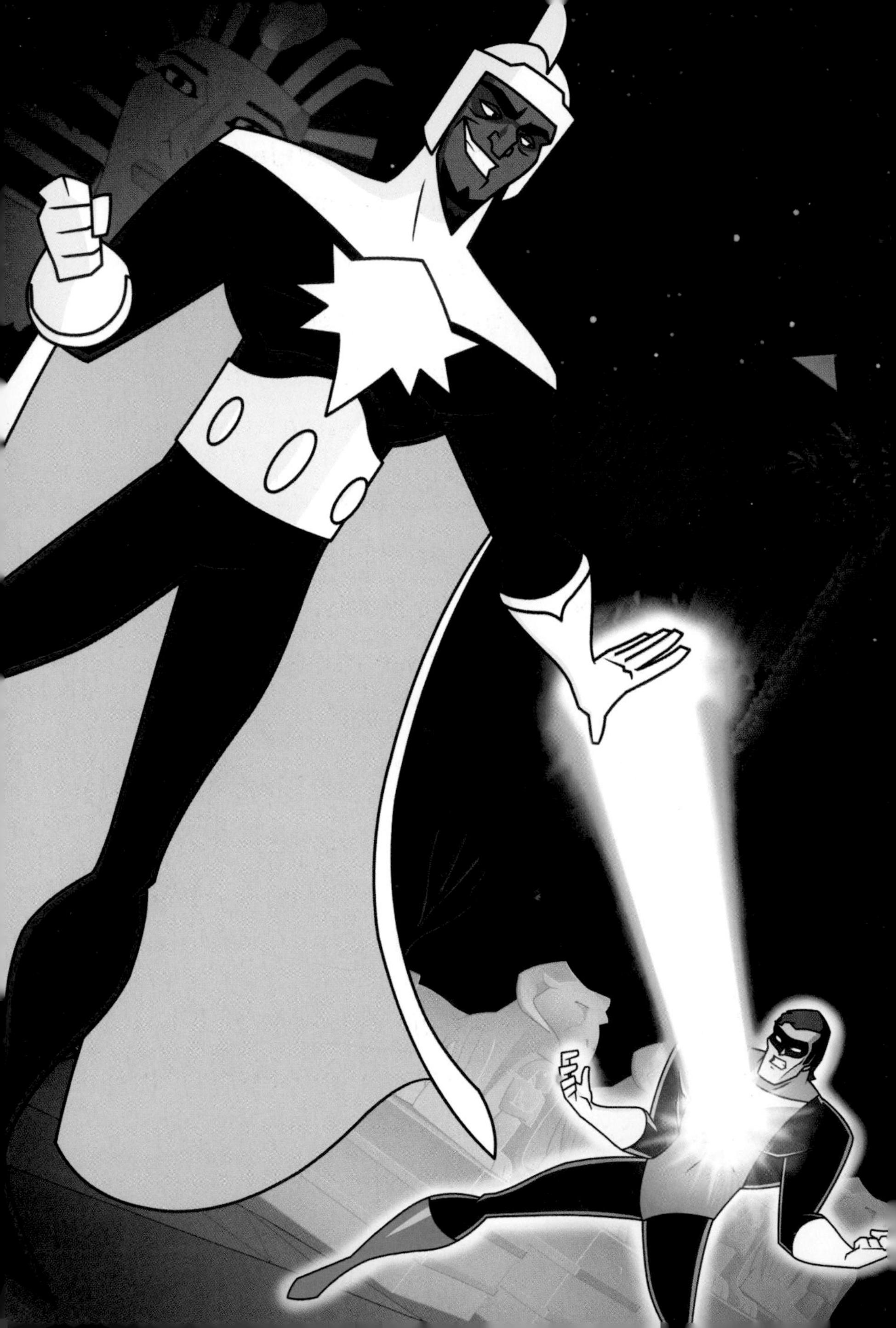

A blinding flash of light exploded in front of Green Lantern. He felt an incredible energy hit him from head to toe. The force knocked him backward onto the city streets. For a split second, Hal lost his concentration on the energy cage, and it disappeared from around Dr. Light.

"I'm stronger than you think!" the villain shouted. "When I'm finished I'll be stronger than any super-villain in the world! I'll be the King of Light!"

THUDDDOMMMMMM!!! Dr. Light threw a bolt of pure white light at his enemy. Regaining his senses, Green Lantern quickly dodged the burst.

"I'm tired of getting no respect!" Dr. Light shouted. "You super heroes think I'm a fool. Even my fellow super-villains think I'm a joke. Well, I'll show all of you!"

He's gone over the edge, Green Lantern thought. *There's only one thing worse than a super-villain, and that's a crazy super-villain!*

Green Lantern commanded his ring to form a straightjacket. He wrapped it around Dr. Light like a cocoon. Then he created a padded cell to imprison the mad marauder.

Suddenly, all the green color drained from the ring's creations. The cell and the straightjacket dissolved like puffs of smoke. Dr. Light was free!

"I control *all* colors of the spectrum," Dr. Light said. "Including the green of your power ring."

A green sword formed in the air in front of Hal. Then a green spear appeared.

Weapons in all the colors of the rainbow surrounded Green Lantern.

"Attack! Attack!" Dr. Light commanded his deadly visions.

The colorful creations zoomed toward Green Lantern. The super hero made a green sledgehammer and swung it in a wide circle. **KKLLAAAANG!** It smashed the sword into pieces and broke the spear in two. The other blades missed Green Lantern the first time but came back for more. Hal created a giant fishing net and scooped up all the weapons.

By then, however, Dr. Light had escaped.

"He sure knows how to make an exit," said Hal. "He's left quite a mess, too."

The entire city of Las Vegas was still in the dark. Tourists screamed with fright.

Green Lantern knew the situation could soon become worse. "I guess it's up to me to turn on the lights," he said.

Hal pointed his ring at a nearby power pole. A dazzling beam of green energy flowed from the ring to its target. A street lamp began to glow. Then the one next to it lit up. Suddenly, the traffic signals began to blink, and the neon hotel lights came on again.

"Warning," the ring said. "Power levels at ten percent."

"Come on, just a little more," Green Lantern pleaded. "The city's electrical grid is almost back to full power."

"Warning! Warning!" the ring repeated. "Power levels at five percent. Failure in twenty seconds. Nineteen . . . Eighteen . . ."

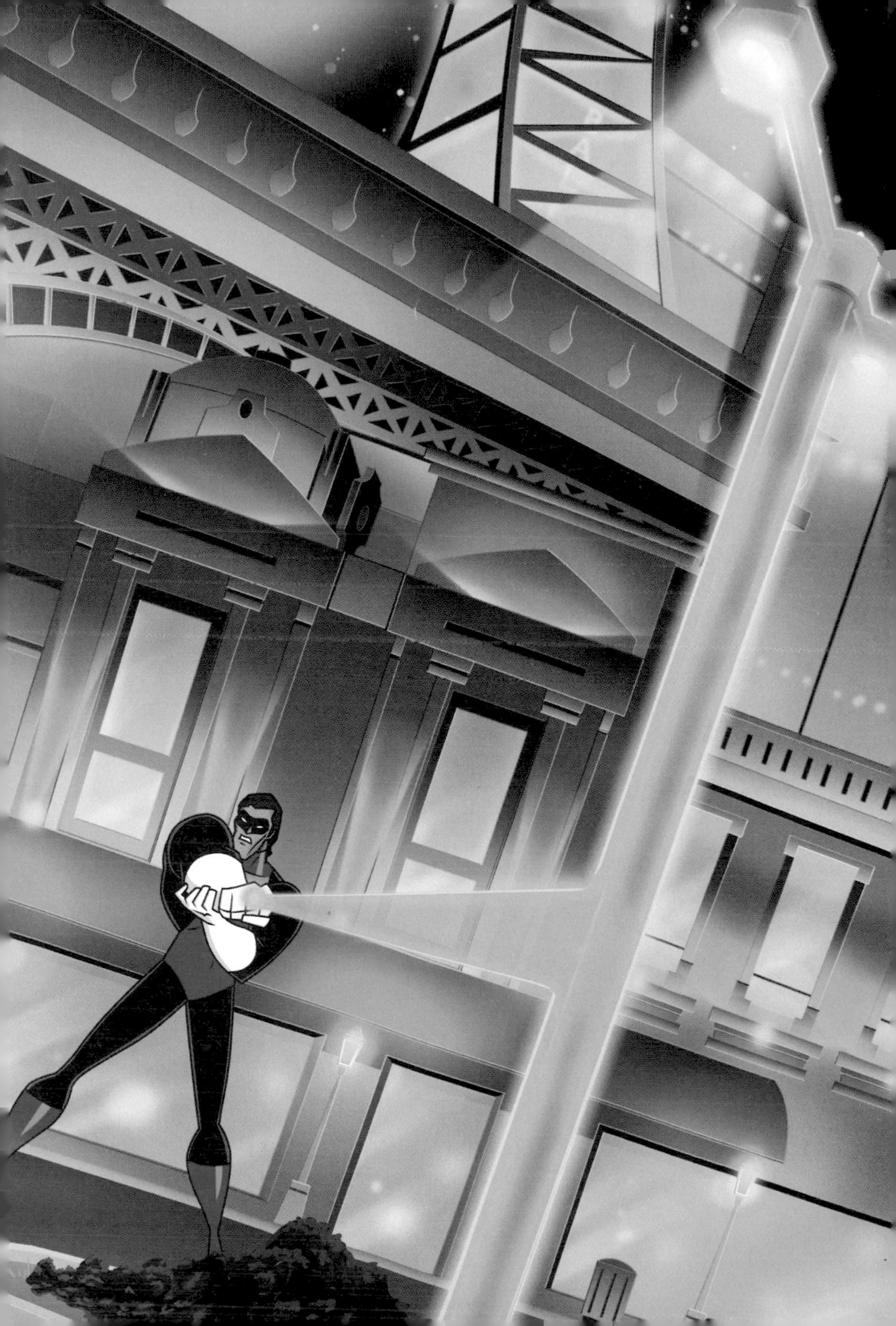

Green Lantern concentrated on his task until the ring went dark. By then, Las Vegas was back to being the brightest city in the world.

"That always tires me out!" Green Lantern said. "But I don't have time to rest. I've got to find the mad doctor."

Green Lantern's ring was out of energy, but not for long. Hal and other Green Lanterns had a way to recharge their superpowered weapons.

Hal Jordan used his will to summon his ring's power source.

An object in the shape of an old-time lantern formed in front of the super hero. He put his ring hand up to one of the lenses. Green light filled the air as Hal recited the Green Lantern Corps oath . . .

"In brightest day,
In blackest night,
No evil shall escape my sight.
Let those who worship evil's might,
Beware my power —

Green Lantern's light!"

When the ring was finished recharging, the Power Battery disappeared. Green Lantern felt strong again. He had been recharged along with his ring.

"Ring, locate Dr. Light," Green Lantern said. "This battle isn't finished!"

CHAPTER 3

ALL FIRED UP

Green Lantern's power ring created a 3-D map, which showed the outline of the United States. On the eastern seaboard of the country, a large X blinked on and off.

"Dr. Light is in New York City," the ring told him.

"I wonder what kind of trouble he's making in the Big Apple?" said Hal.

The super hero didn't think about the question for long. Hal leaped into the night sky. **WHOOOOSH!**

Green Lantern flew at supersonic speed toward New York. It didn't take him very long to reach his destination. Soon, he saw the famous lights of Times Square.

Good, Hal thought. *Dr. Light hasn't gotten here yet —*

Suddenly, the city lights winked out, just as they had done in Las Vegas. Green Lantern formed a spotlight with his ring. The green beam searched the city for Dr. Light and located him atop a tall building.

"Time to knock one out of Central Park!" Green Lantern said. He formed a giant baseball bat and slugged the villain off the building like a tee ball. **THWACK!**

Caught by surprise, Dr. Light tumbled through the air all the way to the Statue of Liberty in New York Harbor.

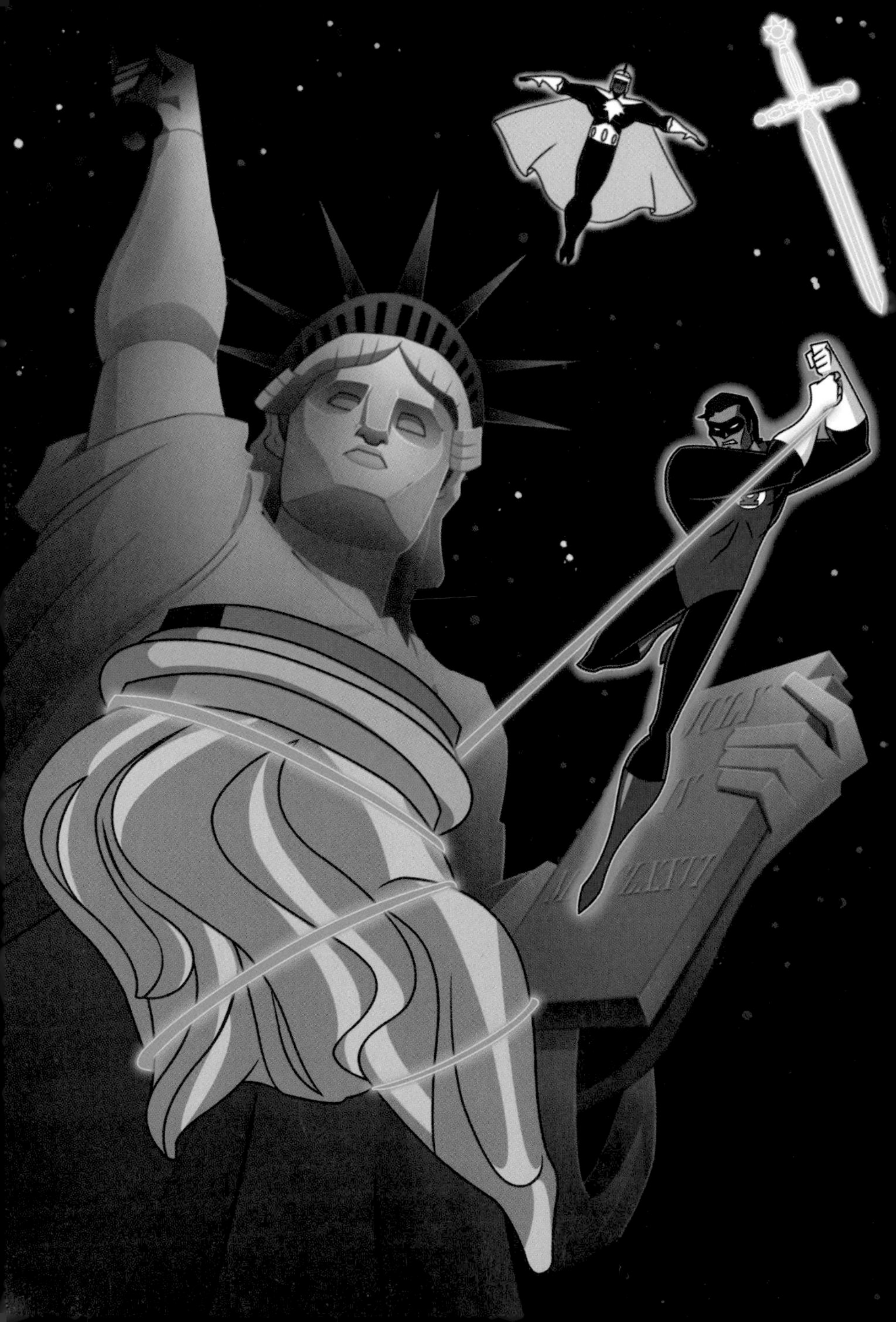

THUD! The villain landed on the historic statue's raised torch.

"The Big Apple was just a snack for me," Dr. Light said. "I've got an appetite for more destruction!"

The villain raised his hand, which glowed with a bright blue light. The light took on the form of a huge sword. Dr. Light swiped the light sword through the metal of Liberty's torch. **CLANK!** The giant fixture began to topple toward the river below.

Green Lantern quickly formed a lasso and caught the torch in midair. Then he pulled the torch back onto its holder in Liberty's hand. Green Lantern used his ring energy to fuse the metal back together. When he looked around, Dr. Light was already gone.

"Dr. Light is heading east," said the super hero's power ring. "Destination unknown at this time."

"No," Green Lantern said, realizing the evildoer's plan. "He's heading for sunlight."

Green Lantern followed Dr. Light's trail across the Atlantic Ocean. It was daytime when he reached the shores of France.

Green Lantern tracked Dr. Light to a small town that had a special building called a solar furnace. Rows of mirrors reflected sunlight onto another giant mirror. That mirror concentrated the sunlight like a magnifying glass. French scientists used the machine's intense heat to melt metal and other materials.

Dr. Light stood in the middle of that hot spot, soaking up the sunlight.

That's the strongest sun beam on the planet, Green Lantern thought. *It will make him more powerful than ever.*

Green Lantern knew he had to get the villain out of the beam. He created a giant green cooking pot and used it to scoop up Dr. Light. Then Green Lantern slammed a lid on it.

"Put a fork in it, Dr. Light. You're done," Hal said with a laugh.

The pot began to shudder and shake. **BANG! BOOM!** It sounded like popcorn popping inside. The lid flew off and balls of light exploded from the container.

"It was dark in there!" Dr. Light yelled. "You know I hate the dark!"

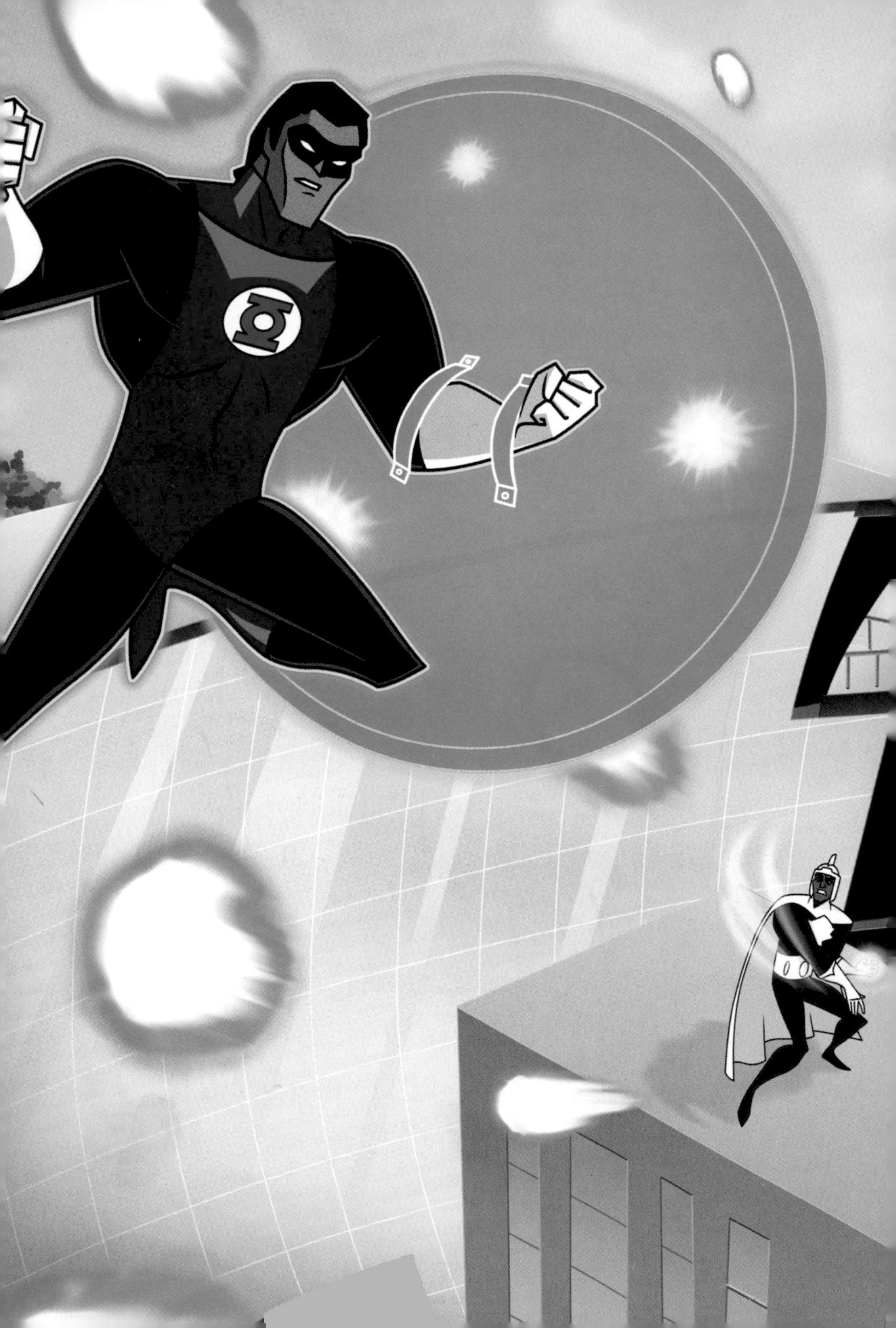

The villain hurled the light balls at Green Lantern like grenades. Green Lantern created a giant gladiator shield to protect himself. **KA-BOOM!** The light grenades exploded against the shield.

"Soon I'll be the master of all the light on the planet!" Dr. Light bragged. "People will speak my name in awe!" The villain was getting stronger by the minute.

They'll call him Dr. Delusional, Green Lantern thought. *He's lost his mind.*

"If I can't remove Dr. Light from the beam, I have to remove the beam from Dr. Light," Green Lantern decided.

The super hero commanded his ring to form an enormous blanket to cover the main mirror. Then he did the same thing to the rows of smaller mirrors.

The light source to the solar furnace went dark. The beam disappeared.

"No!" Dr. Light shouted. "You'll pay for that, Green Lantern!"

Dr. Light's whole body lit up like a flare. The light was so bright that Green Lantern had to shade his eyes. Suddenly, a blast knocked the super hero backward.

He crashed into the big mirror of the solar furnace. The green energy blanket saved Green Lantern from harm, but the mirror was smashed.

"You've ruined my light source!" Dr. Light said. "Now I need another one. It's a good thing I know just where to find it."

CHAPTER 4

S.T.A.R. LIGHT

Green Lantern chased Dr. Light all the way to Metropolis. He wasn't surprised to see that the villain's destination was S.T.A.R. Labs, home of the world's most powerful laser.

Dr. Light blasted his way into the building and didn't stop until he reached the underground laser lab. It was protected by a hundred feet of earth and walls of thick steel. Scientists were working on the laser, but Dr. Light knocked them aside. He stepped in front of the high-tech device.

"I've had to work my way up to this intensity," he said. "First I absorbed the light from the visible spectrum in Las Vegas and New York. Then I absorbed the ultra-violet waves from the sun using the solar furnace. Now one dose from this x-ray laser will make me the master of light on Earth!"

Dr. Light held a bundle of fiber-optic cables in one hand, which controlled the firing commands to the laser. One pulse of light through them would shoot the laser right at Dr. Light. He was ready.

"Now!" the villain shouted.

"No!" another voice said.

A pair of colossal green scissors snipped the fiber-optic cables in two. Then a little green cork plugged the end of the laser barrel. Green Lantern charged into the lab.

WHAM! He hit Dr. Light with a powerful emerald energy blast from his ring.

The super-villain was knocked back into the steel wall. He hit it so hard that he was dazed for a moment. Green Lantern knew that would not last long. He also knew that his ring's creations were not much use against Dr. Light. The villain would only absorb the green light energy.

"Looks like I'm going to have to fight him the old-fashioned way," Green Lantern decided.

Hal gave Dr. Light a stiff punch in the jaw. **THWACK!**

"Ow!" Dr. Light cried, holding up his hands to guard his face.

Green Lantern pulled back his fist for another blow.

"Hitting me is all you can do?" Dr. Light asked.

"No," Green Lantern answered.

A brilliant green beam shot out from his power ring, hitting the floor at Dr. Light's feet. The next thing the villain knew, he was falling into a deep cavern. Green Lantern flew after Dr. Light and used the ring to drill the shaft deeper and deeper. The deeper it got, the darker it got.

I have to get him away from any light, Green Lantern thought. *That's the only way to weaken him.*

Darkness had more than a weakening effect on Dr. Light. He was terrified of the dark. Panic gripped his heart. His fear exploded in a mindless blast of light.

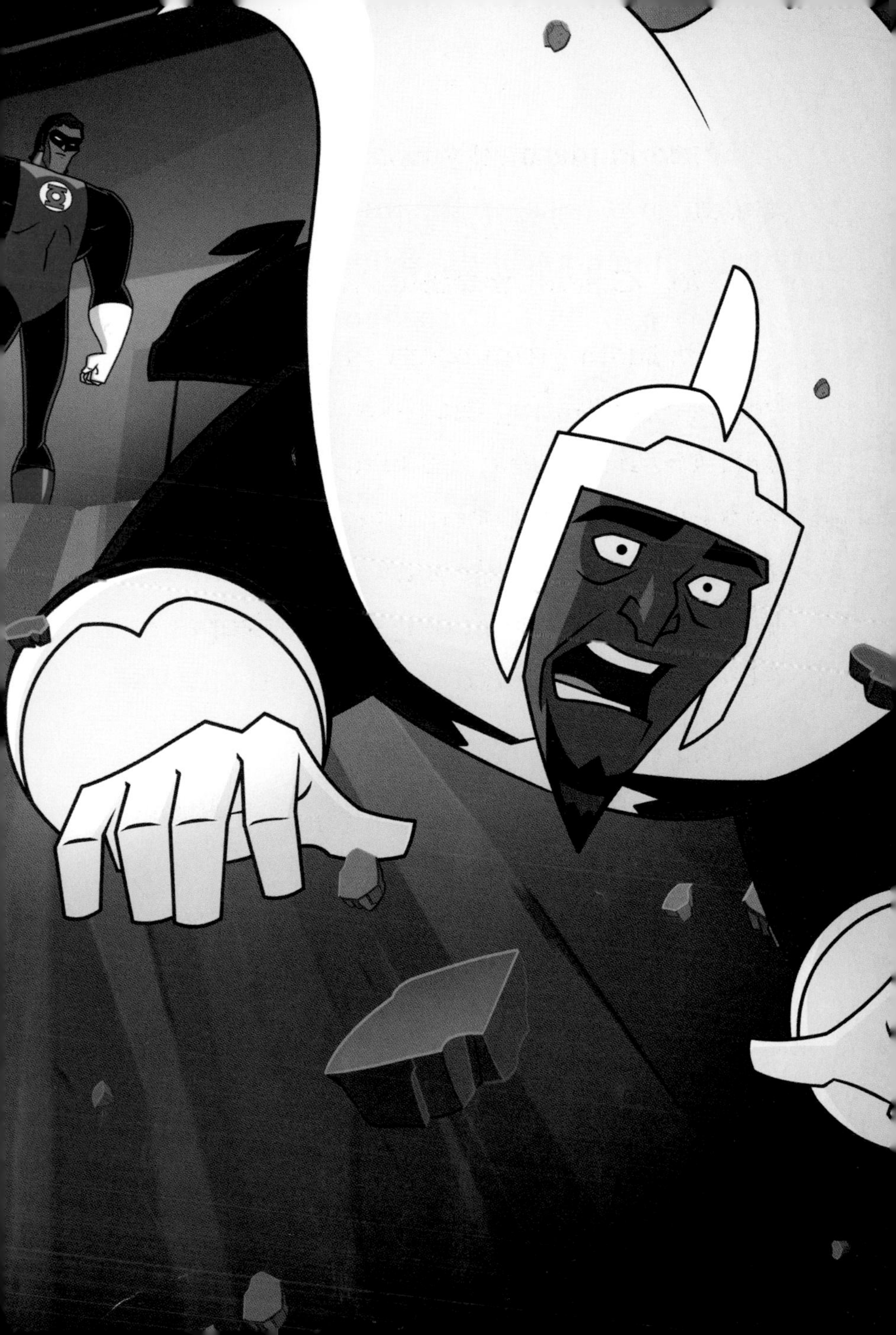

Green Lantern was hit by the blast
and thrown back up the tunnel. The force
hurled him against the ceiling of the lab.
WHAM! He dropped to the floor,
unconscious.

Dr. Light rose out of the pit. "No one will
put me in the dark again!" he shouted.

The crazy criminal walked over to the
laser barrel and picked up the fiber-optic
cables. Green Lantern was knocked out and
could not stop him. The super-villain sent
the command for the laser to fire.

Within moments, Dr. Light absorbed all
of the energy from the pulse of light. He
was filled with strength and confidence.

"Power rings are supposed to be the
most powerful weapons in the universe,"
Dr. Light said. "Not any more!"

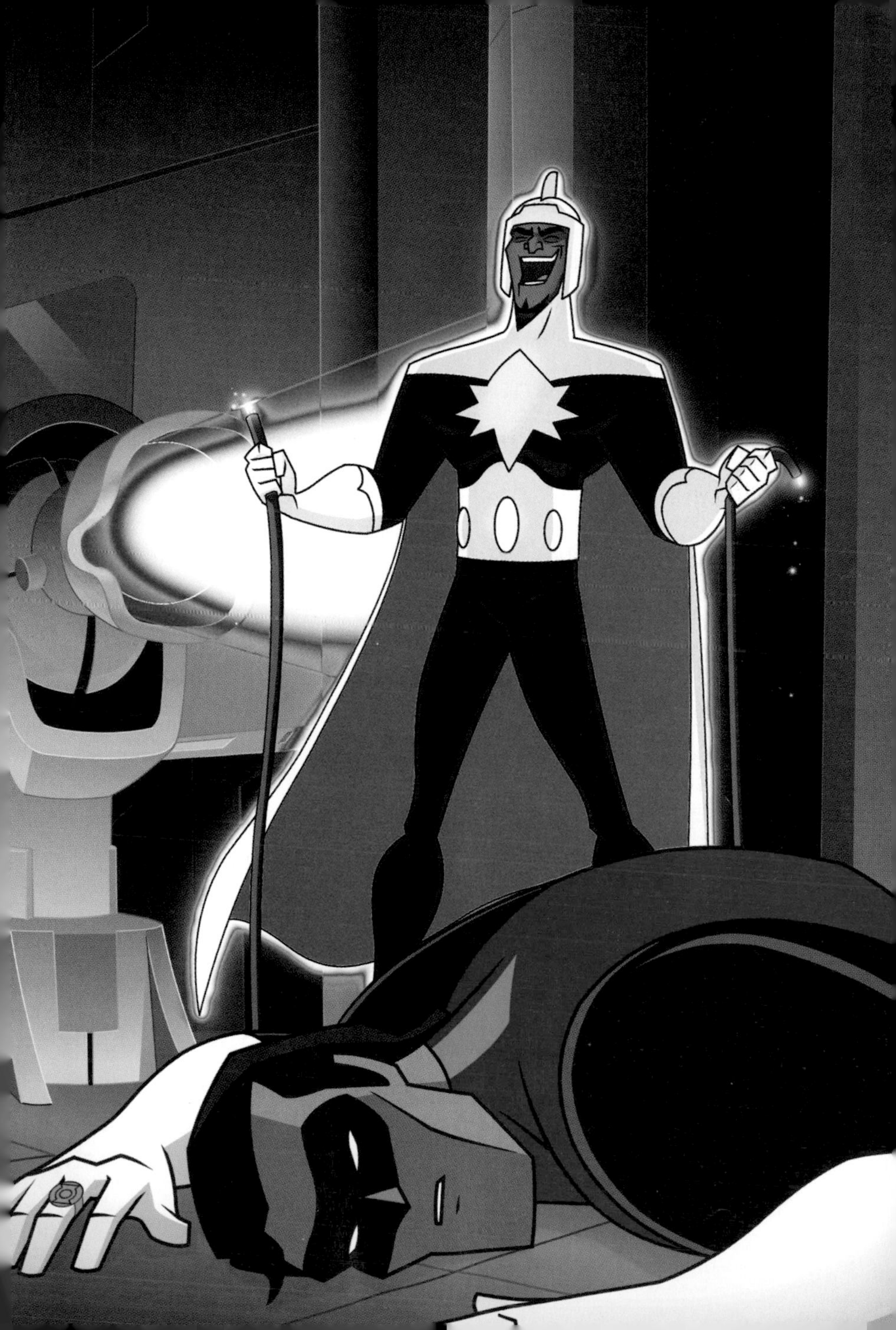

He looked down at the emerald hero lying at his feet. Green Lantern was waking up, but he was still weak.

"I could finish you off, but I won't," Dr. Light said. "I want you to watch as I force the sun to go nova and I absorb all of its light!"

The super-villain laughed.

"There's one last form of light I need before I work up to the sun," he said. "I need the energy from gamma rays. Of course, to get them, I'm going to have to set off a nuclear bomb!"

CHAPTER 5

FINAL CHARGE

Dr. Light was gone when Green Lantern regained his strength. There was a big hole where the villain had smashed through the ceiling. Every ceiling for ten floors up had a hole in it. Green Lantern looked up through the holes and could see the sky.

"Well, Dr. Light sure took the direct route," he said. "But where is he headed?"

"Tracking Dr. Light's flight path," the ring said. "He is heading west."

"Oh no," Green Lantern said.

"I know the closest place he can get his hands on a fully-assembled nuclear bomb," Green Lantern continued. "The nuclear test range in Nevada."

Green Lantern flew through the holes the villain had made in the lab's ceiling. He commanded the ring to give him full speed. He needed to catch up to Dr. Light.

The ring showed Green Lantern how far he was from the villain. The gap was closing quickly. Soon Green Lantern saw a bright glow in the distance. It looked like a flying ball of white flames. Dr. Light!

The super-villain flew over the peaks of the Rocky Mountains. When Hal saw some piles of boulders from landslides, he got an idea. The super hero commanded the power ring to form a giant catapult. Then he used the device to fire boulders at Dr. Light.

CRASH!! The very first boulder knocked Dr. Light out of the sky.

Dr. Light slammed into the side of a mountain. Green Lantern quickly made an enormous green jackhammer to create a rockslide. Dr. Light was buried under a ton of falling stones.

He did not stay down for long. **BOOM!** Dr. Light burst free in a dazzling explosion. The blast sent Green Lantern tumbling across the sky.

By the time Green Lantern arrived at the test range, it was clear that Dr. Light was there. Soldiers with guns were running, tanks were rumbling, and helicopters were in the air. They all gathered around one building. A sign over the front door read: ASSEMBLY. This was where the bombs were built, and Dr. Light was inside.

Green Lantern used the power ring to melt a hole in the roof. Once inside, he saw Dr. Light standing near a large nuclear weapon.

"Don't do this, Light!" Hal said.

"This is my moment of glory!" Dr. Light shouted. "The gamma rays in this bomb will give me the power to blow up the sun!"

"That will kill every person on this planet and wipe out the solar system," Green Lantern pointed out.

"It will make me the master of light for the whole galaxy!" the villain shouted. "Maybe even the universe!"

"So where are you going to rule the universe from if you destroy Earth?" Green Lantern asked. "The nearest planet is twenty light-years away."

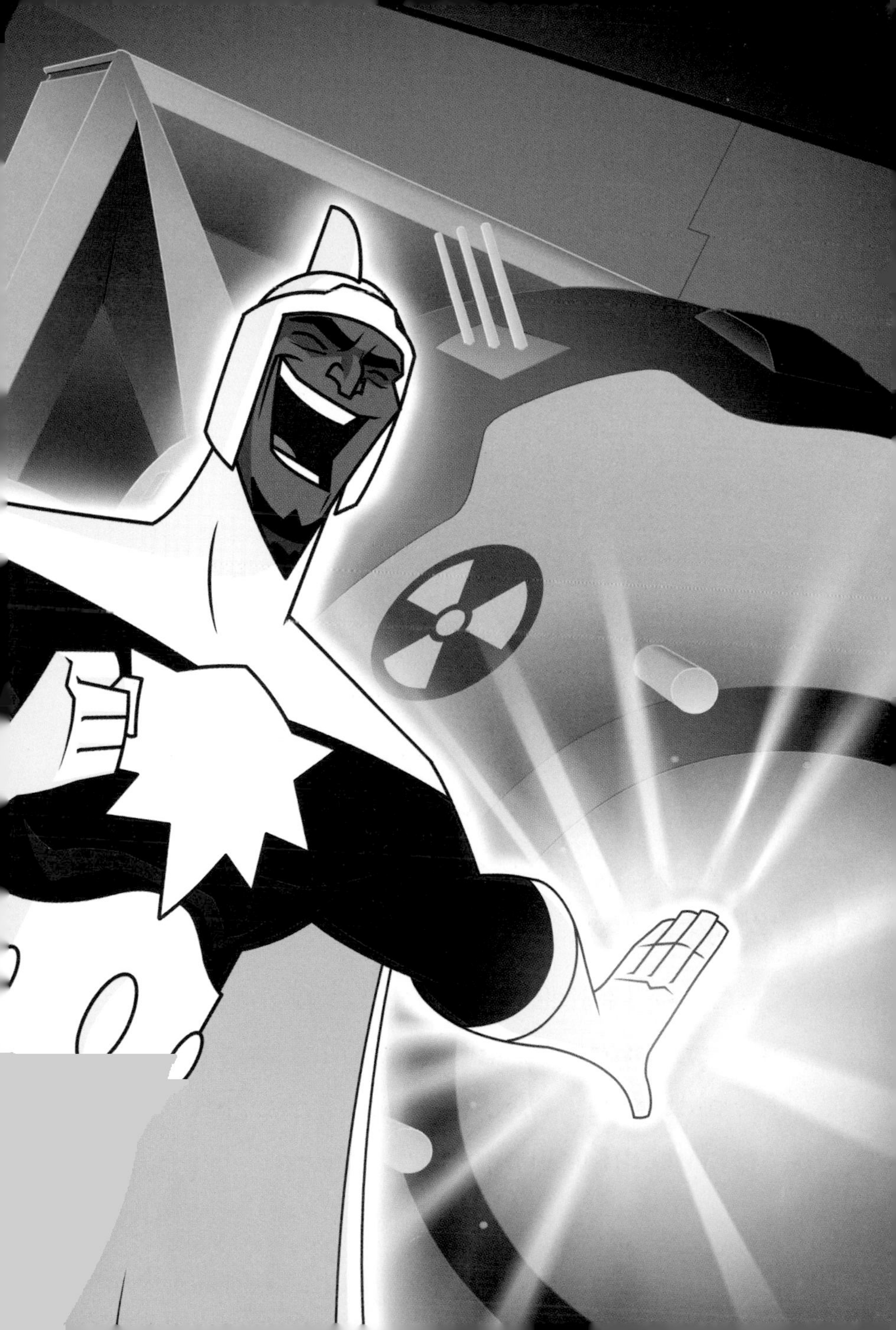

Dr. Light paused.

"I patrol this section of space," Green Lantern said. "I know every moon, asteroid, and habitable world. You don't."

"Then you'll show me!" Dr. Light demanded.

"No. I'll be gone with everyone else on the planet," Green Lantern replied. "You'll be left all alone in space. Can you even survive in space without a ship?"

Dr. Light had not thought of this. The idea of being in the darkness of space scared him. He began to imagine what it would be like.

Green Lantern watched Dr. Light lose concentration. The villain got sucked into his own fear. He was not paying attention, and Green Lantern saw his chance.

Hal formed a green energy sphere around Dr. Light and quickly pumped all the air out of it. The lack of oxygen made Dr. Light faint.

"Pleasant dreams," Green Lantern said.

When Dr. Light woke up, he was still in the green energy sphere. He was about to absorb it when he noticed it was dark outside. There was no light anywhere except the green glow from the sphere.

"Where am I?" he said.

"You're somewhere that the light doesn't shine," Green Lantern said, floating outside of the sphere.

"Am I in space?" the villain squeaked.

"No. You're at the bottom of the ocean," Green Lantern said. "To be specific, you're in the Mariana Trench. It's six miles deep."

"It's so dark," Dr. Light said.

"There's no light for you to absorb," Green Lantern said. "Think of this as your prison. Your sentence is to stay here until you lose your light charge. Then I'll find you a nice, dark jail cell."

"Please! You can't leave me here all alone!" Dr. Light begged.

"I'll be back to check on you," Green Lantern promised. "For now, I'll give you some little friends."

The power ring glowed. It formed three green fish.

Lantern fish.

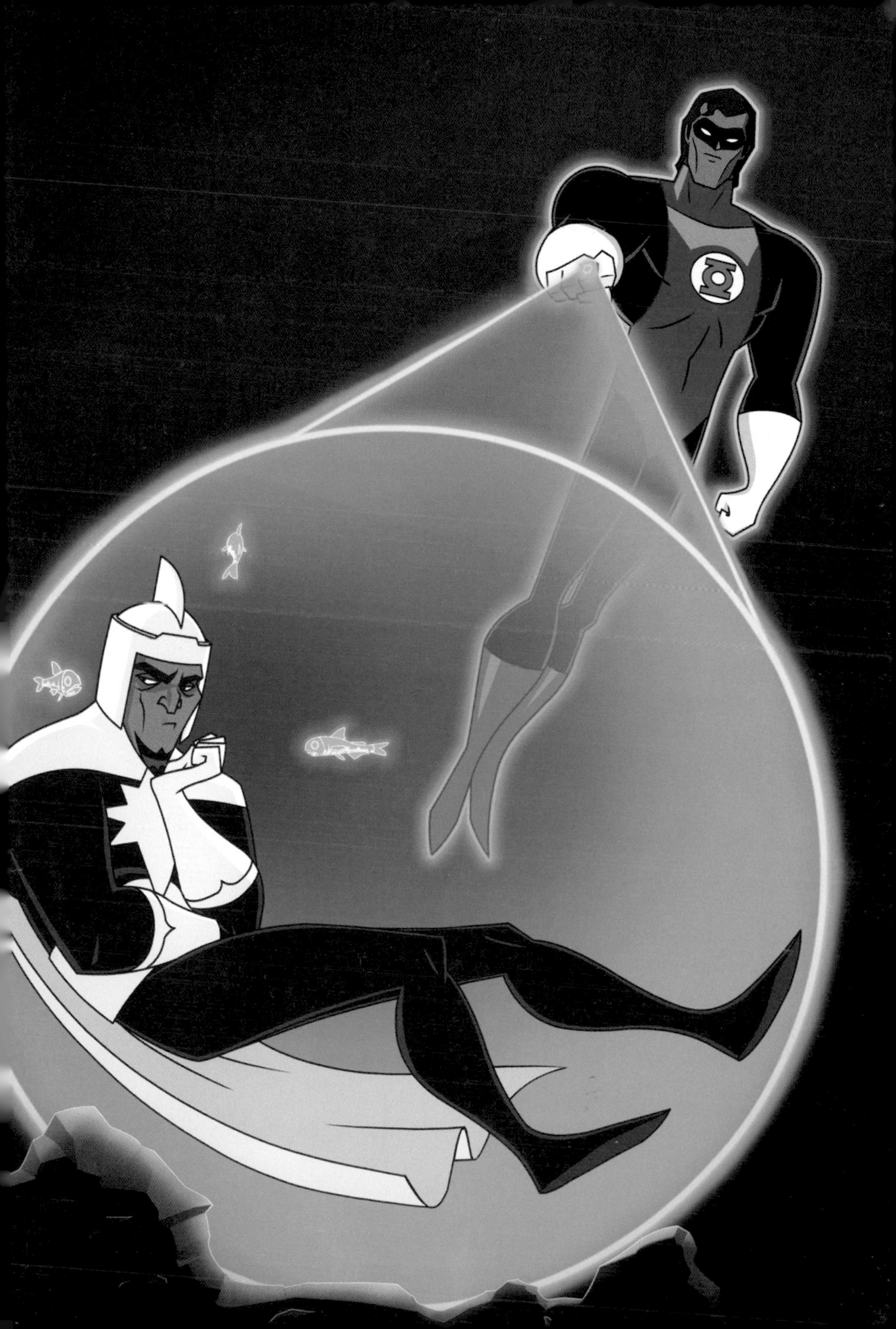

DR. LIGHT

REAL NAME: Arthur Light

OCCUPATION: Criminal

HEIGHT: 5' 11" **WEIGHT:** 171 lbs.

EYES: Black   **HAIR:** Black

POWERS/ABILITIES: Brilliant mind; able to control light for any purpose, including bending light to become invisible, creating powerful energy blasts and force fields; flight.

BIOGRAPHY

While working at S.T.A.R. labs, Dr. Arthur Light and his colleague, Dr. Jacob Finlay, created a powerful, high-tech uniform. Using the suit, which drew energy from light, Finlay attempted to become a super hero. Unfortunately, his experiment failed and Finlay died fighting his first crime. Soon after, Dr. Light donned the invention but decided to use it for a different purpose — to become the world's worst super-villain. After several failures, Dr. Light became trapped inside a Green Lantern power ring. When he escaped, he no longer needed the suit — his body was pure light.

2814

Dr. Light can control anything that emits light, such as a street lamp, the headlights on a car, or a simple flashlight.

Dr. Light has very few weakness. He can drain power from any light source. By scattering light photons, he can also create areas of complete darkness, blinding his enemies.

Dr. Light is also known as the Lord of Luminescence or the Photon Felon.

At first, Dr. Lights powers came from the high-tech suit he created with Dr. Jacob Finlay. However, the super-villain no longer needs this devide to control light.

BIOGRAPHIES

Laurie S. Sutton has read comics since she was a kid. She grew up to become an editor for Marvel, DC Comics, Starblaze, and Tekno Comics. She has written *Adam Strange* for DC, *Star Trek: Voyager* for Marvel, plus *Star Trek: Deep Space Nine* and *Witch Hunter* for Malibu Comics. There are long boxes of comics in her closet where there should be clothing and shoes. Laurie has lived all over the world, and currently resides in Florida.

Dan Schoening was born in Victoria, B.C., Canada. From an early age, Dan has had a passion for animation and comic books. Currently, Dan does freelance work in the animation and game industry and spends a lot of time with his lovely little daughter, Paige.

GLOSSARY

blackout (BLAK-out)—when the lights go out in a town or city because of a power failure

concentrated (KON-suhn-tray-tuhd)—made something stronger by focusing the energy

corps (KOR)—a group of people acting together

fiber optic (FYE-bur OP-tik)—bundles of extremely thin glass or plastic tubes through which light passes

guardian (GAR-dee-uhn)—someone who guards or protects something

spectrum (SPEK-truhm)—the range of colors that is revealed when light shines through a prism or drops of water, as in a rainbow

straitjacket (STRAYT-jak-it)—a coat made of strong material that can be used to restrain a harmful person

supersonic (soo-pur-SON-ik)—faster than the speed of sound

willpower (WIL-pou-ur)—the ability to control what you will and will not do

DISCUSSION QUESTIONS

1. Sometimes Hal must choose between saving an innocent person and stopping the villain. Which choice would you make and why?

2. What do you think of Hal's punishment for Dr. Light? Can you think of any other ways to punish this super-villain?

3. Each Lantern color is powered by an emotion. What emotion best describes you? Is your emotion a power or a weakness? Explain.

WRITING PROMPTS

1. This story takes place in the city of Las Vegas. Write a story about Dr. Light and Green Lantern that takes place in your town. What would happen to your school and your house? Describe.

2. Green Lanterns have unmatched willpower, the ability to control what they will and will not do. Write about three things that you must use willpower to avoid. Do you crave candy? Are video games hard to resist? Describe.

3. Do you think a Green Lantern could ever be defeated? Write down how you would take on a Green Lantern and win.

MORE NEW GREEN LANTERN ADVENTURES!

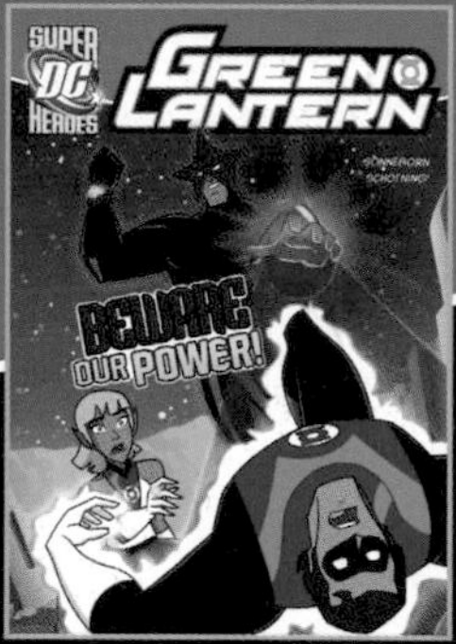
SUPER DC HEROES
GREEN LANTERN
BEWARE OUR POWER!
BEWARE OUR POWER!

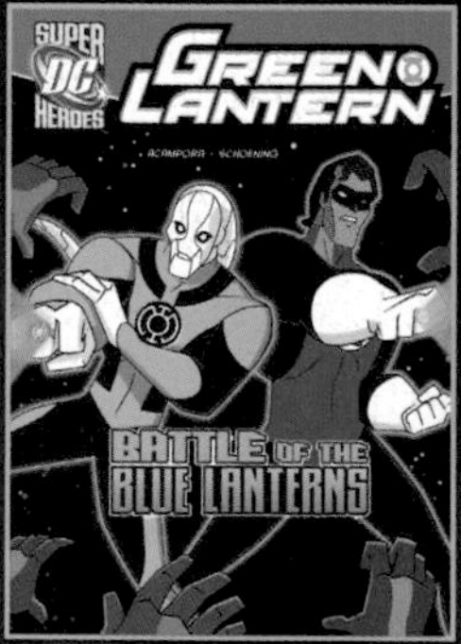
SUPER DC HEROES
GREEN LANTERN
BATTLE OF THE BLUE LANTERNS
BATTLE OF THE BLUE LANTERNS

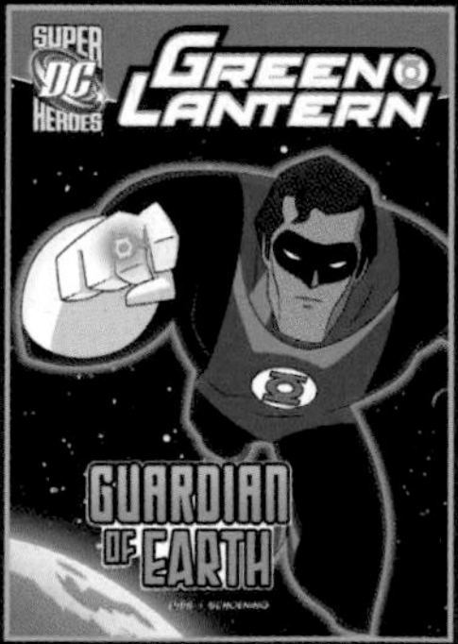
SUPER DC HEROES
GREEN LANTERN
GUARDIAN OF EARTH
GUARDIAN OF EARTH

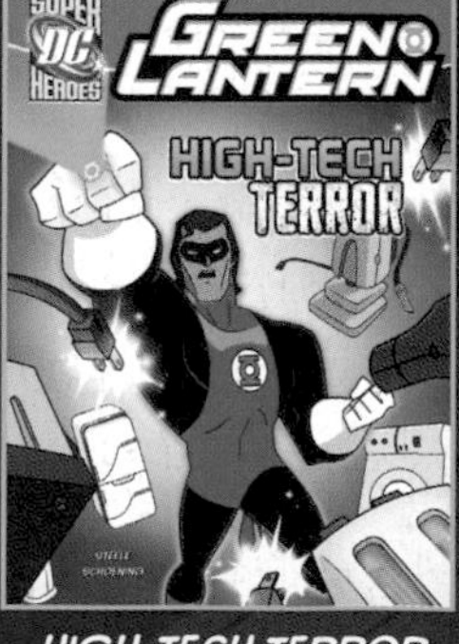
SUPER DC HEROES
GREEN LANTERN
HIGH-TECH TERROR
HIGH-TECH TERROR

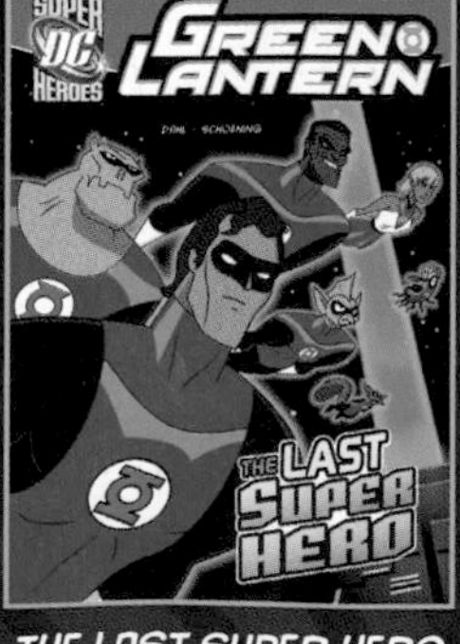
SUPER DC HEROES
GREEN LANTERN
THE LAST SUPER HERO
THE LAST SUPER HERO

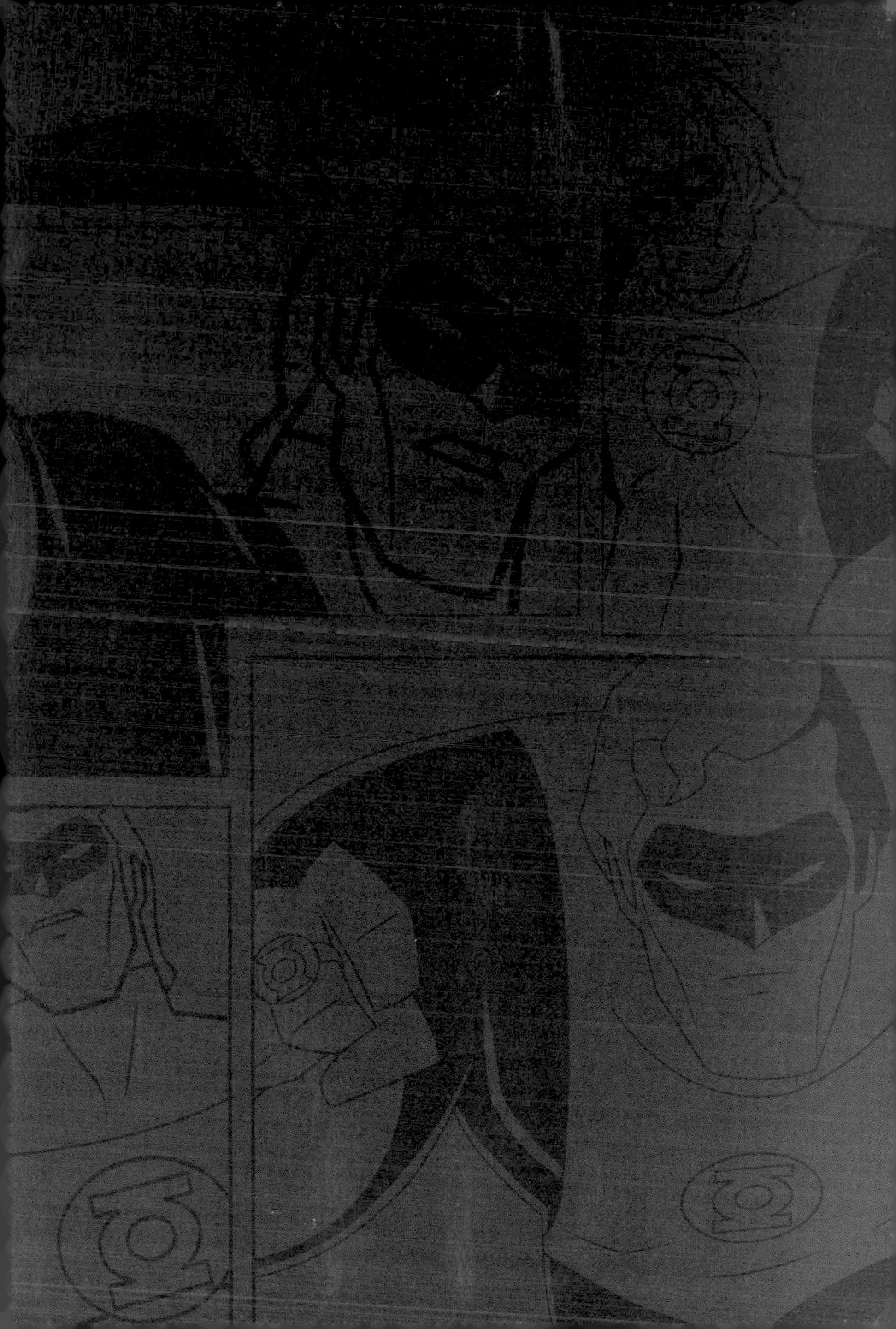

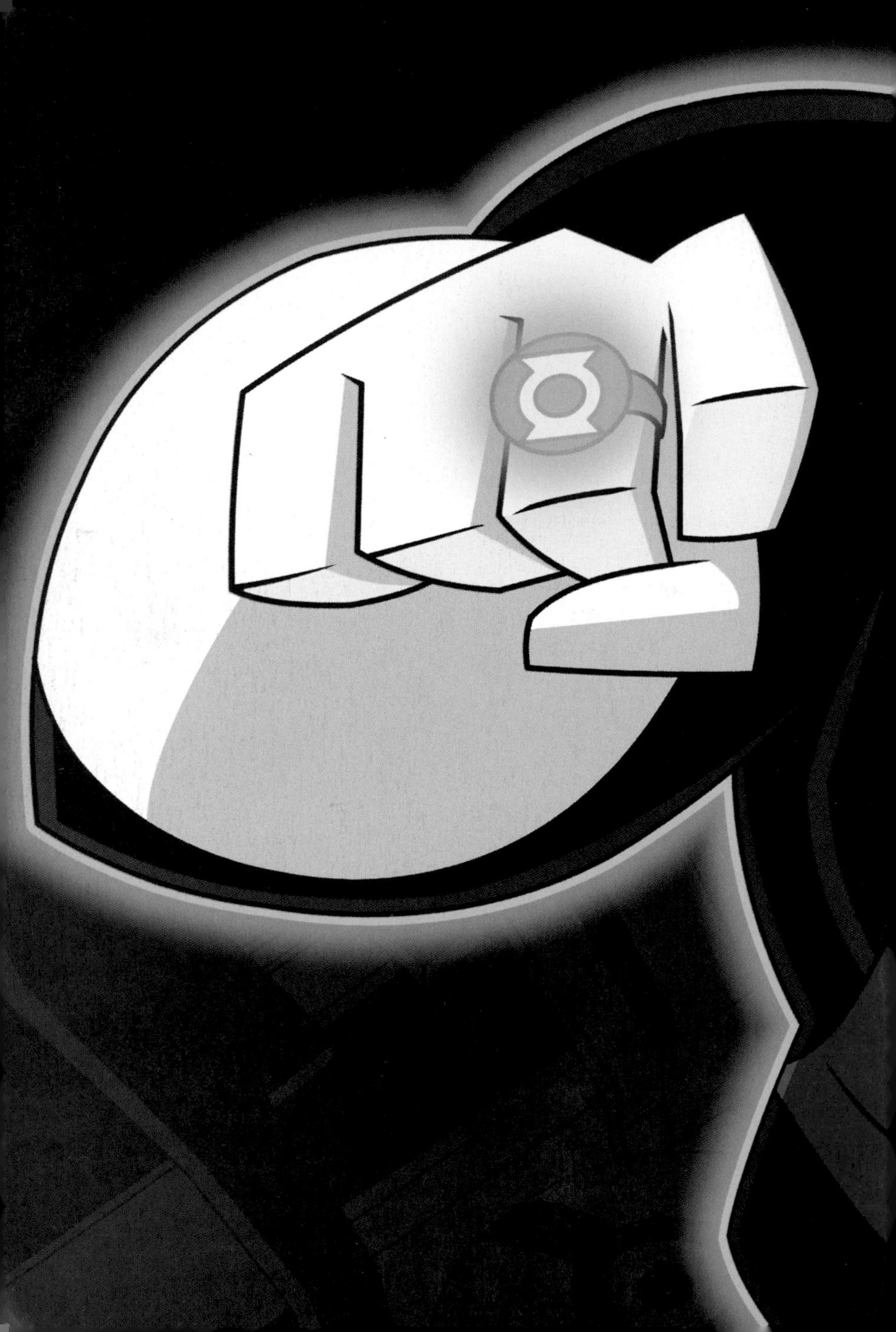

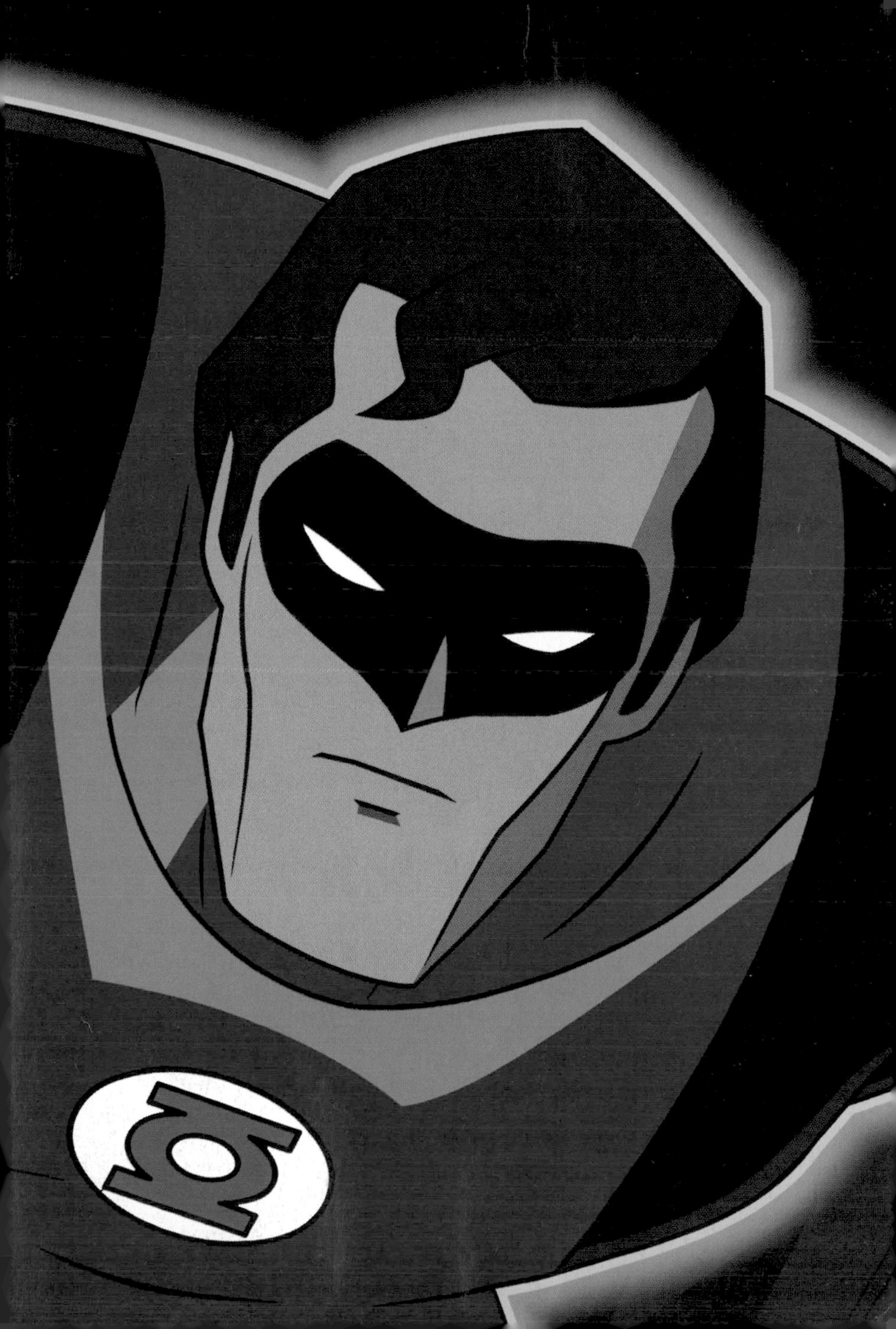